In honor of my mom and dad, who always did their civic duty —M.M.

To Mrs. Player's class, making a better tomorrow every day —M.P.

Visit us on the Web! rhcbooks.com
Educators and librarians, for a variety of teaching tools, visit us at RHTeachersLibrarians.com

Library of Congress Cataloging-in-Publication Data
Names: McNamara, Margaret, author. | Player, Micah, illustrator.
Title: Vote for our future! / Margaret McNamara; Micah Player.
Description: First edition. | New York City: Schwartz & Wade Books, [2020] |
Summary: The students of Stanton Elementary School, which is a polling place, find out all they can about voting
and then encourage everyone in their neighborhoods to cast their ballots.
Identifiers: LCCN 2019007530 | ISBN 978-1-9848-9280-5 (hardcover) | ISBN 978-1-9848-9281-2 (hardcover library binding) |
ISBN 978-1-9848-9282-9 (ebook)
Subjects: | CYAC: Voting—Fiction. | Political participation—Fiction. | Elections—Fiction.
Classification: LCC PZ7.M47879343 Vot 2020 | DDC [E]—dc23

The text of this book is set in Century Schoolbook
The illustrations were rendered digitally.
Book design by Micah Player and Rachael Cole

MANUFACTURED IN CHINA
2 4 6 8 10 9 7 5 3 1
First Edition

VOTE ★ for ★ OUR FUTURE!

by
MARGARET McNAMARA

illustrations by
MICAH PLAYER

schwartz & wade books · new york

Every two years, on the Tuesday after the first Monday of November . . .

. . . Stanton Elementary School closes for the day.

For repairs?

Nope!

For a holiday?

Nuh-uh.

For vacation?

No way!

Stanton Elementary
School closes for . . .

ELECTION DAY and changes from a school to a POLLING STATION!

What's a polling station?

A polling station is where people vote.

The reason people vote is to choose who makes the laws of the country.

"We should all vote!" said LaToya.
"We should all vote to make the future better."

"We can't vote until we turn eighteen," said Lizzy.

"So what can we do?"

The kids of Stanton Elementary School did their research.

They looked in books and made notes.

They went online and found all kinds of information.

They even took a trip to their local
election office and picked up forms.

VOTER GUIDE

VOTER GUIDE

INFORMATION

"I can't wait till
I can vote for real,"
said Amal.

VOTER GUIDE

"Me either!" said everybody else.

"Kids have to live with adult choices!"

The kids of Stanton
Elementary School were
ready to spread the word.

Cady and her mom made flyers
and handed them out.

"Don't forget to vote,"
Cady told one busy dad.

"I didn't even know there
was an election," he said.

VOTE for OUR FUTURE!

"Now you do!" said Cady.

"Can I go with you when you vote?" Jasmine asked her big sister.

"It's a pain to vote," her sister said.

"I'm not even registered," added her friend.

"It's not hard to register!" said Jasmine. "You can do it together, and I can show you how."

Nadiya and her auntie went door to door.

"Voting is a right!" Nadiya said.

"A right that women didn't have a hundred years ago."

One lady told them, "I don't like standing in lines."

"I don't like lines either," answered Nadiya's auntie, "but if we stand in line for coffee, or for a movie, or at a bank . . ."

". . . I bet we can stand in line to vote!" said Nadiya.

"Hmmm," said the lady. "Maybe we can."

At Jayden's house, the whole family was making their voting plans. Jayden's dad was voting before work. Jayden's mom was voting after work.

"I've walked to that polling station every election since I could vote," Jayden's great-gran told him. "But I can't walk so far anymore."

"A volunteer can drive you!" said Jayden.
"Let's get you set up," said Jayden's mom.

Mia and Noah and Jamal had a bake sale.

"Don't forget to vote!" Mia said
as she handed out change.

BE
SWEET
and
VOTE

"I'll be away on Election
Day," said one woman.
"In our state you can
vote early!" said Mia.

VOTING
is a
PIECE
of
CAKE

"Or you can vote by mail,"
said Jamal. "The Voter Guide
tells you how."

"Voting! What's the big deal?" asked a teenager.

"People fought wars so we can vote," said Mia. "That's a big deal."

DONUT forget TO VOTE

VOTER GUIDE

"Why should I vote?" said a sad lady. "Nothing ever changes. Besides, one vote won't make a difference."

"Are you kidding?" said Jamal. Changes are made every day because people voted.

COUNTS!

They rolled in on wheelchairs.

They voted for the first time
and for the fiftieth time.

. . . voters came early in the morning, before the sun was up.

They waited in line, with coffee.

By the time it was the first Tuesday after the first Monday of November, every kid at Stanton Elementary School had spread the word

to their families,

to their neighbors,

to friends,
to strangers,

to friends of strangers.

The whole town
had a voting plan.

And on Election Day . . .

They came with their sons and daughters, their nieces and nephews, their brothers and sisters, their cousins and friends.

They ran in at the last minute.

On the first Wednesday after the first Monday of November,
all the votes had been counted.

The results were so close, the votes had to be counted again.

Some people won,

and some people lost.

The laws of the country began to change.

Stanton Elementary School went back to being a school.

And the future began to change.

GET OUT THE VOTE!

When adults vote, they vote for people and causes they believe in. They vote so that those who speak for us—our local and state representatives, our congresspeople, our president—will follow policies and make laws that are good for everyone in the country.

Acts of Congress are laws that have to be followed by everyone in the United States of America. Here are some Acts of Congress that made the future better:

The **Postal Service Act** was signed into law by our nation's first president, George Washington, in 1792. It established the United States Post Office Department. Nowadays, the US Postal Service delivers over 140 *billion* pieces of mail.

Before the **Civil Rights Act** was passed in 1866, people who had been enslaved had no rights at all. This was the first Act of Congress to make it a law that every citizen be treated equally. Americans still struggle to preserve every person's civil rights today.

The **Yellowstone National Park Protection Act** became a law in 1872. Now there are national parks in every US state and territory, consisting of over eighty million acres, preserved for the benefit and enjoyment of the people.

The **Indian Citizenship Act** became law in 1924. Although this law granted citizenship to all indigenous people, many Native people did not have the ability to vote until 1962.

The **Air Pollution Control Act of 1955** was the first law to declare that air pollution was a national problem.

The **Civil Rights Act of 1964** was signed as a result of the civil rights movement. This law made it a crime to "injure, intimidate, or interfere with . . . any person . . . because of [their] race, color, religion, sex, handicap . . . familial status . . . or national origin. . . ." It continues to be amended to protect the rights of all.

The **Americans with Disabilities Act,** passed in 1990, states that people who are differently abled must be accommodated in schools, in the workplace, and in public spaces.

The Patient Protection and Affordable Care Act was passed in 2010. It ensures that all people in the United States have access to health care at an affordable cost.

WHEN YOU CAST YOUR FIRST VOTE, what KIND OF FUTURE WILL YOU VOTE FOR?